USBORNE HOTSHOTS
SEASHORE

USBORNE HOTSHOTS
SEASHORE

Edited by Mandy Ross
Designed by Rachel Wells and Karen Tomlins

Illustrated by John Barber
and Ian Jackson

Series editor: Judy Tatchell
Series designer: Ruth Russell

Consultant: Margaret Rostron

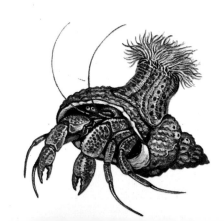

CONTENTS

Searching for seashore life

This book shows some of the thousands of strange and beautiful creatures you can find on the seashore, surviving storms, salt spray, wind and sun. How many types (or species) of animals and plants can you spot there? You can record your findings in the chart on pages 30-31.

Tides and tidal zones

Every day, the sea level rises and falls. These changes are called tides. In every 24 hours, there are two high tides (when the sea reaches its highest level) and two low tides (the lowest point).

To live between high and low tide levels, plants or animals must be able to withstand the waves and currents. They must also be able to survive both in and out of sea water.

The area above the high tide mark is called the splash zone.

The upper shore is underwater only at high tide. Few plants or animals live here.

The middle shore is underwater about half the time.

The lower shore is only uncovered at low tide. Lots of plants and animals live here.

Measuring

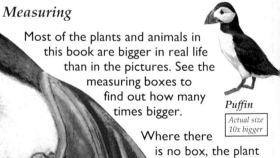

Most of the plants and animals in this book are bigger in real life than in the pictures. See the measuring boxes to find out how many times bigger.

Puffin

Actual size
10x bigger

Where there is no box, the plant or animal is shown actual size.

Here is the actual size of a puffin's head.

4

Where the sea meets the land

There are four main kinds of beaches: rocky, sandy, muddy and shingle. You will find different kinds of plants and animals on each.

Rocky shores are rich in plants and animals. Look on the rocks for shelled animals and seaweeds, and in rock pools for fish, crabs, starfish and sea anemones.

Rocky shore

Sandy and muddy shores are good places to watch wading birds — and the burrowing crabs, shellfish and worms which they feed on.

Sandy shore

Little can grow on a shingle beach, as the pebbles are constantly being shifted by the sea. But you will find seaweed and lots of shells washed ashore.

Shingle beach

What lives where?

Most species of plants or animals in this book can be found on the coasts of Europe and North America.* A few species are included which live only on warmer shores — for instance the Mediterranean Sea.

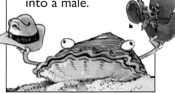

Did you know..?

A young flatfish looks like an ordinary fish. As it settles down on the seabed, its body flattens out — and slowly, one eye moves around its head, so that both are on the top side.

This eye has moved over the fish's head.

A Flounder camouflaged against the sand

Eels migrate up to 7,500km (4,700 miles) from European or American waters to breed in the Sargasso Sea.

An oyster starts life as a male, and slowly changes into a female. After laying her eggs, she changes back into a male.

*Tropical shores, and the Pacific coast of America, are especially rich in animals and plants. You will find lots of other species there in addition to those in this book.

Crabs

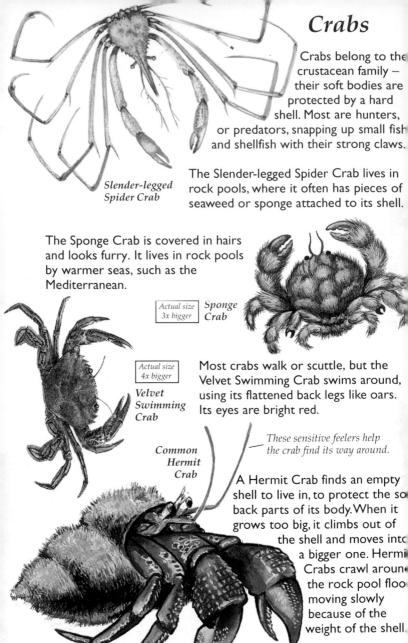

Crabs belong to the crustacean family — their soft bodies are protected by a hard shell. Most are hunters, or predators, snapping up small fish and shellfish with their strong claws.

Slender-legged Spider Crab

The Slender-legged Spider Crab lives in rock pools, where it often has pieces of seaweed or sponge attached to its shell.

The Sponge Crab is covered in hairs and looks furry. It lives in rock pools by warmer seas, such as the Mediterranean.

Actual size 3x bigger

Sponge Crab

Actual size 4x bigger

Velvet Swimming Crab

Most crabs walk or scuttle, but the Velvet Swimming Crab swims around, using its flattened back legs like oars. Its eyes are bright red.

Common Hermit Crab

These sensitive feelers help the crab find its way around.

A Hermit Crab finds an empty shell to live in, to protect the soft back parts of its body. When it grows too big, it climbs out of the shell and moves into a bigger one. Hermit Crabs crawl around the rock pool floor moving slowly because of the weight of the shell.

While the tide is out, Shore Crabs hide in the mud, safe from sea birds. Young Shore Crabs often have attractive markings on their shell.

Shore Crab

Large, hairy claws

Porcelain Crabs are very small. They hide under stones and seaweed on the lower shore.

Tiny back legs

Porcelain Crab

Eyes on stalks

The Toad Crab has a pear-shaped shell. It withdraws its eyes into sockets to protect them from danger.

Toad Crab

Actual size
4x bigger

The Thornback Spider Crab gets its name from its spiny shell.

Thornback Spider Crab

Actual size
7x bigger

Actual size
2x bigger

Edible Crab

Large Edible Crabs live in deep water, but small ones are common in rock pools or buried under sand on the lower shore.

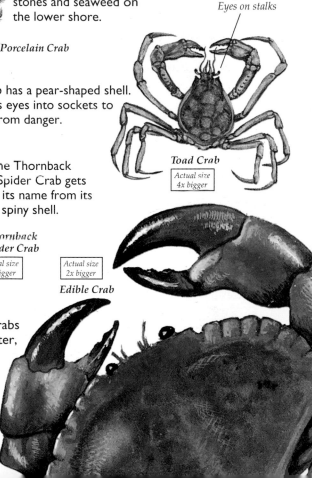

Lobsters, shrimp and small fry

All these hard-shelled animals are crustaceans, like their relatives, crabs. Shrimp and prawns are hard to spot because their bodies are almost transparent. You may find colonies of barnacles clinging to rocks below the high tide mark.

Your best chance of seeing a lobster is to watch fishing boats unload their catch. Lobsters crawl along the seabed in deep waters, looking for dead fish to eat.

Actual size
2x bigger

Plated Lobster

Common Lobster

Actual size
4x bigger

Like all crabs and lobsters, the Plated Lobster has ten legs, but the last, small pair is usually hidden under its shell.

Barnacles

Acorn Barnacles

Barnacles produce a kind of glue to cement themselves to rocks or other hard surfaces. They don't need to move from the spot, because once they are covered by water, they put out feathery limbs to filter tiny plants to eat from the water.

A barnacle's feathery limbs extend from the opening in its shell.

Prawns are larger than shrimp, and their feelers are longer than their bodies. The Common Prawn is found in shallow water and rock pools.

Prawns have a beak-like snout, called a rostrum.

Actual size 2x bigger

Common Prawn

Camouflaged against seaweed

Chameleon Prawn

The Chameleon Prawn changes from blue at nighttime to red, green or brown in the daytime, so it can hide in seaweed from predators. It may be found in deep rock pools.

Shrimp spend the summer in river estuaries, but return to the seashore in winter. They burrow into the sand, leaving their feelers poking out to sense the tiny creatures which they prey on.

Common Shrimp

Shrimp's feelers are shorter than prawns'.

Sea Slaters look like giant sow bugs. They hide in crevices in the rock high on the shore, and scuttle around at high speed to find food.

Sea Slater

Gribbles tunnel through waterlogged wood, for instance pier supports, and leave tiny holes.

Gribbles

Sandhoppers jump when they are disturbed. They live under stones, and crawl around at the high tide mark, scavenging for seaweed. Birds such as Turnstones feed on Sandhoppers.

Sandhoppers up to 2cm (¾in) long

Shells

All the empty shells on the beach once belonged to living creatures, called mollusks. Mollusks have soft bodies with no legs, and they grow a shell for protection against sea birds or other predators looking for a snack. If you search hard, you may find the living animals clinging to seaweed or rocks.

A Painted Topshell (above) can be yellow, pink or white with red streaks.

Gastropods

All the shells on these two pages belong to the snails of the seashore, called Gastropods. Inside the shell, the animal's body has a muscular foot that clings to rocks or seaweed.

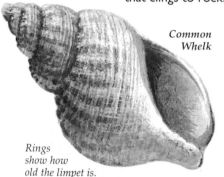

Common Whelk

Dog Whelks hunt other shelled animals. First the Dog Whelk climbs onto the shell and drills a hole. Then it sucks out the soft parts of the animal inside.

Dog Whelk

Rings show how old the limpet is.

Limpets clamp themselves firmly to boulders to withstand battering tides and predators' attacks. They move around in the dark at low tide to feed on seaweed.

Blue-rayed Limpets feed on seaweed, weakening the plant by chewing into its stem.

Blue-rayed Limpet

Common Limpet

Slipper Limpet

Up to nine Slipper Limpets live in a chain, one on top of another – females at the bottom and males on top.

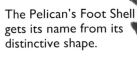

The Pelican's Foot Shell gets its name from its distinctive shape.

Common Periwinkle

Pelican's Foot

Shaped like a webbed foot

Periwinkles feed on seaweeds. Flat Periwinkles can be yellow, orange, brown or striped.

Flat Periwinkle

Necklace Shell

Common Cerith

Hermit crabs sometimes live in empty Ceriths.

Like the Dog Whelk, this creature is a predator.

Tropical shells

You might see cowries and other exotic tropical shells for sale. In the past, certain cowrie shells were used as money in parts of India and the Pacific.

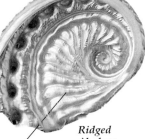

Ridged Abalone

Actual size 2x bigger

Mother-of-pearl lining inside shell

Cowrie

Spines stop the shell from sinking into sand.

This Spider Stromb belongs to the Conch family. If you hold a conch to your ear, some people say you can hear the sea.

Actual size 3x bigger **Spider Stromb**

11

Bivalves

The shells, or mollusks, on this page are bivalves, which means they have two shells hinged together with muscles. Most of these shelled animals filter their food from sea water.

Scallops move around by clapping their two shells together, forcing water out behind to jet themselves along.

Queen Scallop

Mussel

You can buy shellfish such as Scallops, Oysters and Mussels as seafood. Shellfish absorb harmful chemicals from polluted water, so to avoid food poisoning, people are careful to gather them only from clean places.

Oyster

Actual size 4x bigger

All the mollusks below burrow into the sand to hide from hungry sea birds. Each one digs with a muscular foot that it can poke out of its shell.

Actual size 3x bigger

Blunt Gaper

Baltic Tellin

Cockle

Muscular foot

Razor Shells look like barbers' old fashioned razor blades. They use their foot to burrow as deep as 1m (3ft) into the sand.

Razor Shell *up to15cm (6in) long*

Razor Shell burrowing

Muscular foot

Soft bodies and tentacles

All these soft-bodied creatures are mollusks. Sea Slugs – like slugs on land – have no shell at all. They have tentacles on their heads and often have bright markings to warn predators that they taste horrible.

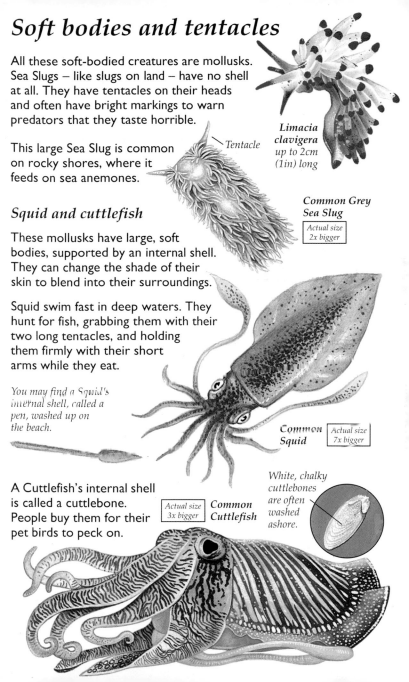

Limacia clavigera
up to 2cm
(1in) long

This large Sea Slug is common on rocky shores, where it feeds on sea anemones.

Tentacle

Common Grey Sea Slug

Actual size
2x bigger

Squid and cuttlefish

These mollusks have large, soft bodies, supported by an internal shell. They can change the shade of their skin to blend into their surroundings.

Squid swim fast in deep waters. They hunt for fish, grabbing them with their two long tentacles, and holding them firmly with their short arms while they eat.

You may find a Squid's internal shell, called a pen, washed up on the beach.

Common Squid

Actual size
7x bigger

A Cuttlefish's internal shell is called a cuttlebone. People buy them for their pet birds to peck on.

Actual size
3x bigger

Common Cuttlefish

White, chalky cuttlebones are often washed ashore.

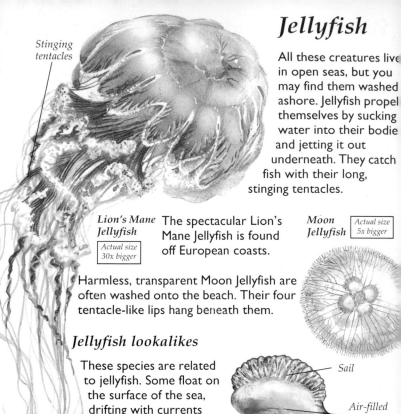

Stinging
tentacles

Jellyfish

All these creatures live in open seas, but you may find them washed ashore. Jellyfish propel themselves by sucking water into their bodies and jetting it out underneath. They catch fish with their long, stinging tentacles.

Lion's Mane Jellyfish

Actual size 30x bigger

The spectacular Lion's Mane Jellyfish is found off European coasts.

Moon Jellyfish

Actual size 5x bigger

Harmless, transparent Moon Jellyfish are often washed onto the beach. Their four tentacle-like lips hang beneath them.

Jellyfish lookalikes

These species are related to jellyfish. Some float on the surface of the sea, drifting with currents and the wind.

A Portuguese Man-o'-War can give you a painful sting. All its tentacles are separate creatures, living as a colony.

Sail

Air-filled float

Portuguese Man-o'-War

Actual size 5x bigger

Shoals of By-the-Wind Sailors are blown across the surface of the sea.

By-the-Wind Sailor

Sea Gooseberry

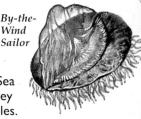

The strong-swimming Sea Gooseberry catches prey with its two long tentacles.

Worms

These seashore worms are related to the earthworms who live in soil. Some stay in one place for most of their lives, while others swim around in search of food.

Bootlace Worms lie coiled under muddy shingle. The longest one ever found measured 55m (60yd) – as long as five buses end to end!

Bootlace Worm

Wormcast on sand

Lugworm in its U-shaped burrow

Lugworms suck in sand and digest any edible scraps. Then they pass the sand out, leaving a wormcast on the surface. They can grow as long as 15cm (6in).

Keelworm peeping out of its tube

Keelworms build themselves hard, ridged tubes to live in. Look for them on rock surfaces and shells.

The hairy Sea Mouse belongs to the worm family, but it looks a little like a mouse if you see it swimming in the water.

Sea Mouse

Actual size 2x bigger

Clam Worm up to 10cm (4in) long

Bristles

Clam Worms are predators, snapping up small creatures in their flexible jaws. They also filter tiny edible scraps from mud and water. Their bristles help them to burrow in the sand.

15

Sea anemones and sponges

Sea anemones and sponges are animals, even though they could be mistaken for delicate plants. Sea anemones are related to jellyfish and they hunt in the same way, using their stinging tentacles to capture food such as shrimp and prawns.

Snakelocks Anemones are large enough to catch small fish with their purple-tipped, sticky tentacles.

| Actual size 2x bigger | *Snakelocks Anemone* |

Mouth

A Beadlet Anemone, open under the water.

It closes at low tide to avoid drying out.

Beadlet Anemones (left) are common in rock pools. They survive at low tide by drawing in their tentacles and closing their mouth. They can be red, brown or green.

Dahlia Anemones' warty bodies can get covered with pieces of broken seashell – so they are hard to spot in rock pools.

Dahlia Anemone

| Actual size 3x bigger |

Feathery tentacles

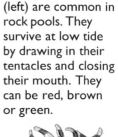

Plumose Anemone

The Plumose Anemone is orange or white. You may see it growing on pier supports, just below the water surface.

16

The anemone grips the shell with a sucker on its base.

The Hermit Crab Anemone lives with a hermit crab, protecting it by fending off predators with its stinging tentacles. In return, it can feed on the crab's leftover food.

Daisy Anemones grow in cracks in the rock. Their tentacles float on the water.

Daisy Anemone

Actual size 2x bigger

Hermit Crab Anemone

Sponges

Sponges are very primitive animals. They pump sea water through their bodies, digesting any tiny edible scraps. If you press a sponge, it will squirt water out.

The green or yellow Breadcrumb Sponge crumbles like bread when handled. It grows on the rocky lower shore.

Breadcrumb Sponge

Sea Orange

Actual size 3x bigger

Like some sea anemones, the Sea Orange grows on a hermit crab's shell. It camouflages the crab, and in return the crab transports it to fresh feeding grounds.

Dead Men's Finger Coral

Actual size 2x bigger

Dead Men's Finger Coral

Corals are another group of plantlike animals. Most coral colonies grow in tropical seas, where they form large coral reefs. Colonies of Dead Men's Fingers, though, are found in cooler waters, submerged or washed ashore.

Starfish and sea urchins

Starfish and sea urchins are all related. Each of these spiny, headless animals has its mouth on the underside of its body.

Starfish

Most starfish have five arms, with rows of suckers underneath which they use to move around on. If an arm breaks off, they can grow a new one.

Sunstar

The Sunstar has up to 13 arms. It preys on other starfish.

Brittlestars are common, but hard to spot under stones in rock pools. Their long, thin arms break easily.

Brittlestars

Spiny Starfish are armed with hard spines against predators like sea snails and fish.

Spiny Starfish

Actual size 6x bigger

The tips of its arms turn up when it starts to move.

In deep waters, Common Starfish can grow up to 50cm (18in) across. On the beach, though, you are likely to find smaller ones.

This starfish is using its powerful suckers to force open a shell and eat the creature inside.

Common Starfish

Cushion Star

Actual size 3x bigger

Short-armed Cushion Stars are common in shady rock pools.

The Brown Serpent Star prefers warmer coasts. The stripes on its arms darken with age.

Striped, spiny arms

Brown Serpent Star

The shell, or test, of a dead sea urchin

Sea urchins

A sea urchin eats with the five teeth on the base of its body, scraping small plants, called algae, off the rocks.

A living Edible Sea Urchin (left) has spines all over its round shell. The spines drop out when the animal dies. You may find its empty shell, called a test, on the beach.

Edible Sea Urchin

Actual size
7x bigger

Sea Potato

Actual size
4x bigger

The Sea Potato is a kind of sea urchin. It burrows deep in the sand, where it is protected from predators.

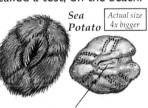

A Sea Potato's test, or empty skeleton, is so light it is blown around on the beach.

Purple-tipped Sea Urchins are more common than their larger relatives, Edible Sea Urchins.

Purple-tipped Sea Urchin

Black Sea Urchin

Common Mediterranean Sea Urchin

These two Sea Urchins prefer warmer seas. Both grow up to 10cm (4in) across.

Seaweeds

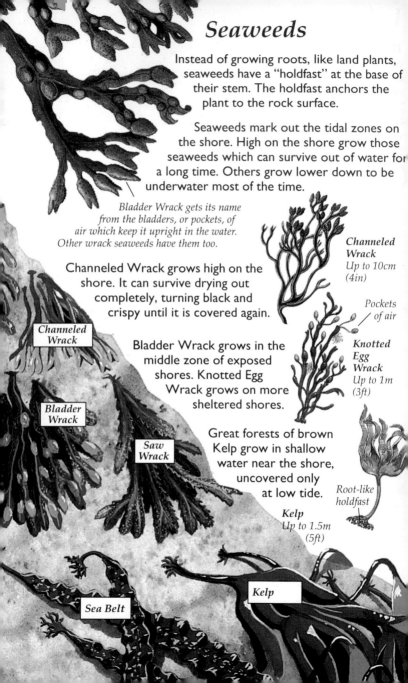

Instead of growing roots, like land plants, seaweeds have a "holdfast" at the base of their stem. The holdfast anchors the plant to the rock surface.

Seaweeds mark out the tidal zones on the shore. High on the shore grow those seaweeds which can survive out of water for a long time. Others grow lower down to be underwater most of the time.

Bladder Wrack gets its name from the bladders, or pockets, of air which keep it upright in the water. Other wrack seaweeds have them too.

Channeled Wrack grows high on the shore. It can survive drying out completely, turning black and crispy until it is covered again.

Bladder Wrack grows in the middle zone of exposed shores. Knotted Egg Wrack grows on more sheltered shores.

Great forests of brown Kelp grow in shallow water near the shore, uncovered only at low tide.

Channeled Wrack
Up to 10cm (4in)

Pockets of air

Knotted Egg Wrack
Up to 1m (3ft)

Root-like holdfast

Kelp
Up to 1.5m (5ft)

Channeled Wrack

Bladder Wrack

Saw Wrack

Sea Belt

Kelp

Red seaweeds like Edible Dulse can live underwater in deep rock pools where the light is very poor.

Edible Dulse
Up to 30cm (1ft)

Sea Lace grows in shallow water. Its thin, graceful cords can grow as long as 6m (6½yd).

Sea Lace

Wavy fronds of Sea Lettuce are common on the rocky lower shore. It grows darker with age.

Sea Lettuce
Up to 50cm (18in)

Gut Laver's fronds are tube-shaped. It is common high on the shore and in river estuaries.

Gut Laver
Up to 20cm (8in)

Eel Grass leaves have a glossy covering to keep salty water out.

Large banks of Eel Grass grow in river estuaries and sheltered sea coasts. Flocks of Brent Geese feed on it during their winter stay in Northern Europe.

Eel Grass

Leaves up to 1m (3ft)

Flowers

Seed pod

To survive the buffeting winds and salt spray, seashore flowers need to grow close to the ground or send down deep, sturdy roots.

California Poppy

Actual size 2x bigger

Yellow Horned Poppy

Actual size 2x bigger

The Yellow Horned Poppy gets its name from its long seed pods. Its deep roots anchor it firmly on shingle beaches. Closely related, California Poppies grow on America's Pacific coast.

Sea Campion thrives on shingle beaches, growing afresh whenever it is uprooted by storms.

Sea Campion

Actual size 3x bigger

Thrift can survive in salty spray. It grows in springy cushions on rocky beaches or low on sea cliffs. It has narrow leaves to reduce water loss.

Thrift

Actual size 2x bigger

Blueweed flowers are bright and eye-catching. In the past, people thought the leaves could cure snake bites.

Bird's Foot Trefoil gets its name from its three-part leaf, like a bird's foot.

Sea Holly's prickly leaves have a waxy coating to stop the plant from drying out.

Sea Rocket survives being buried in shifting sands.

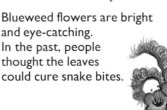

Blueweed

Sea Rocket

Sea Bindweed grows low and trailing, to reduce the risk of being blown away by strong winds.

Sea Bindweed

Sea Lavender grows on land often flooded by the sea, called salt marshes.

Sea Lavender

Actual size 7x bigger

The Sea Aster is a member of the Daisy family. It is also common on salt marshes.

Sea Aster

Actual size 40x bigger

Tough roots of Couch Grass and Marram Grass bind shifting sands into dunes. Then other plants can take root there too.

White Clover and Ragwort can survive by the seashore, but you will find them growing in lots of other places too.

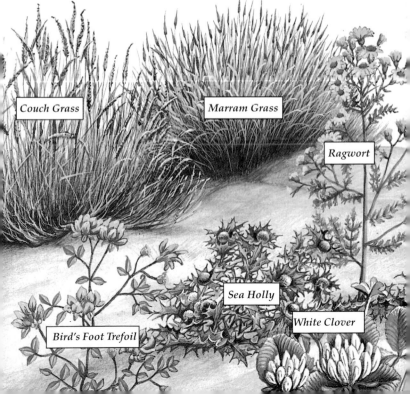

Couch Grass

Marram Grass

Ragwort

Sea Holly

White Clover

Bird's Foot Trefoil

Waders and gulls

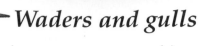

On these two pages are some of the wading birds who dig in the sand or mud to find worms and shellfish. Gulls swoop and shriek overhead, or squabble for scraps on the quay.

Redshank

Actual size
5x bigger

Flocks of Shelducks are common in Europe. They often nest in old rabbit holes in the sand dunes.

Shelduck

Actual size
15x bigger

Orange-red legs give the Redshank its name.

The Curlew is unmistakeable with its long, curved beak and bubbling cry. In spring it breeds on open grasslands, but it spends the winter by the shore.

Curlew

Actual size
10x bigger

Terns have long wings and tails. They dive into the sea to catch sand eels and other fish.

Groups of Oystercatchers feed at the shoreline. Their black and white markings flash as they fly.

Common Tern

Oystercatcher

Sanderling

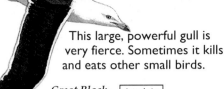

This large, powerful gull is very fierce. Sometimes it kills and eats other small birds.

Great Black-Backed Gull

Actual size 18x bigger

Kittiwakes are a kind of gull. They sometimes follow fishing boats in the hope of a meal.

Actual size 15x bigger **Kittiwake**

Ringed Plover

Actual size 8x bigger

Male Ringed Plovers make a striking flight display in the spring, circling and calling to attract a mate.

Turnstones have a short beak, squat body and a strong neck for turning over stones in search of food.

Ringed Plover

Turnstone

Waders' beaks

Each kind of wader feeds in a different way, according to the length of its beak. This means they can all find enough to eat without competition.

Turnstones search for small crabs and sandhoppers living on the surface.

Shelducks scoop up tiny snails with their short beaks.

Redshanks probe the sand with medium length beaks.

Oystercatchers have strong beaks for prying open shellfish such as mussels.

Curlews probe for deep-burrowing creatures like lugworms.

Pelicans' beaks have a large, soft pouch for scooping up fish. Pelicans live in warmer climates on American shores.

Cliff birds

During the breeding season in spring and early summer, rocky cliffs are alive with birds and their noisy young. Each species, or type, of bird makes its nest at a particular height. The cliffs are deserted the rest of the year, though, as the birds migrate or feed out at sea.

Manx Shearwaters feed at sea, and fly back to their cliff top burrows at night for safety. They are easy to spot as they are white underneath and black on top.

Manx Shearwater

Actual size 12x bigger

Puffin

Actual size 12x bigger

Puffins use their beaks to dig nest holes, usually on grassy cliff tops in colder climates.

Actual size 12x bigger

Fulmar

You can spot Fulmars because they fly with very straight, stiff wings.

Gannet

Actual size 25x bigger

Catching fish out at sea, Gannets dive headfirst from a great height, making an enormous splash.

Razorbill

Actual size 15x bigger

A Razorbill lays a single egg in its nest of seaweed scraps in a crack in the rock.

Guillemot

Actual size 15x bigger

Guillemots perch on bare cliff ledges. Their eggs are pear-shaped so they spin around rather than rolling off the cliff.

Cormorant

Actual size 20x bigger

Shags and Cormorants' feathers are not waterproof, so you may see them holding their wings out to dry!

Shag

Actual size 20x bigger

Mammals

Clumsy on land, seals are graceful acrobats in the water. Like dolphins and porpoises, they are mammals – so they need to swim to the surface for air.

Grey Seals gather in small herds on rocky shores. They are noisy and sometimes aggressive, hissing, hooting and snarling.

Actual size
35x bigger

Grey Seal

Herds of Harbor Seals live on sandbanks and river estuaries. The pups can dive and swim almost from birth.

Actual size
40x bigger

Harbor Seal

Sea Lions are related to seals, but their back feet make them more agile on land. They are common on America's Pacific coast.

Actual size
50x bigger

California Sea Lion

Dolphins and porpoises

Dolphins and porpoises sometimes swim very close to the shore, but you are most likely to spot them from a boat.

Bottle-nosed Dolphin

Actual size
25x bigger

Dolphins are sociable creatures, swimming in groups, or schools, of up to a thousand. They prefer warm seas, although they visit northerly shores occasionally.

Dolphins leap playfully out of the water.

Actual size
25x bigger

Common Porpoise

Porpoises are smaller than dolphins. They eat squid and small fish such as herring.

Fish

Lots of predators – birds, foxes and even badgers – come angling for a meal in shallow seashore waters. So fish use all kinds of defenses, such as slippery skin, camouflage and poisonous spines. Try spotting fish in rock pools. You'll need to be patient, as they dart into hiding at a passing shadow or a sound.

Corkwing Wrasse

Actual size 3x bigger

Corkwing Wrasses are common in warmer waters. They start life as females, and become male with age.

Flounder

Actual size 12x bigger

Flatfish like Flounder hide by flapping their bodies into the sandy seabed. They can change their markings to blend in with their surroundings.

Poisonous spines

In warmer waters, the Scorpion Fish hunts by night for other fish, crabs and prawns.

Scorpion Fish

Actual size 4x bigger

Greater Pipefish

Actual size 5x bigger

Pipefish are very hard to see, camouflaged among seaweed or eel grass. The male carries eggs in a groove under its body until they hatch.

Pipefish and Sea Horses are related. Their snouts are a similar shape.

Sea Horses swim by waving their fin in a rippling movement.

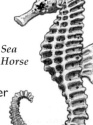

Sea Horse

Sea Horses live in warmer seas, clinging to seaweed with their curved tails.

28

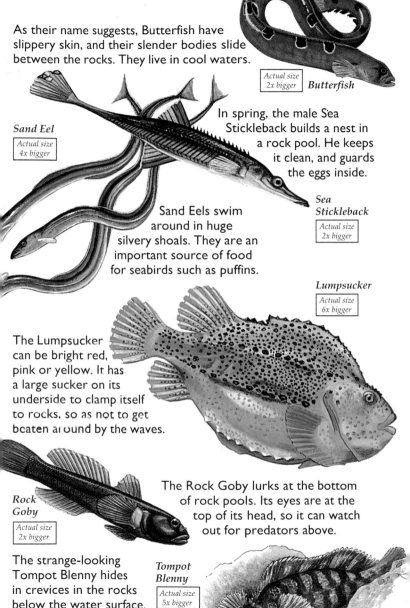

As their name suggests, Butterfish have slippery skin, and their slender bodies slide between the rocks. They live in cool waters.

Actual size 2x bigger | *Butterfish*

Sand Eel

Actual size 4x bigger

In spring, the male Sea Stickleback builds a nest in a rock pool. He keeps it clean, and guards the eggs inside.

Sand Eels swim around in huge silvery shoals. They are an important source of food for seabirds such as puffins.

Sea Stickleback

Actual size 2x bigger

Lumpsucker

Actual size 6x bigger

The Lumpsucker can be bright red, pink or yellow. It has a large sucker on its underside to clamp itself to rocks, so as not to get beaten around by the waves.

Rock Goby

Actual size 2x bigger

The Rock Goby lurks at the bottom of rock pools. Its eyes are at the top of its head, so it can watch out for predators above.

The strange-looking Tompot Blenny hides in crevices in the rocks below the water surface.

Tompot Blenny

Actual size 5x bigger

29

Spotter's chart

All the plants and animals shown in this book are listed here in alphabetical order. When you spot one, you can record it by marking the box beside its name and filling in the date.

	X	Date seen		X	Date seen
Acorn Barnacle			Common Shrimp		
Baltic Tellin			Common Squid		
Beadlet Anemone			Common Starfish		
Bird's Foot Trefoil			Common Tern		
Black Sea Urchin			Common Whelk		
Bladder Wrack			Corkwing Wrasse		
Blueweed			Cormorant		
Blue-rayed Limpet			Couch Grass		
Blunt Gaper			Cowrie		
Bootlace Worm			Curlew		
Bottle-nosed Dolphin			Cushion Star		
Breadcrumb Sponge			Dahlia Anemone		
Brittlestar			Daisy Anemone		
Brown Serpent Star			Dead Men's Finger Coral		
Butterfish			Dog Whelk		
By-the-Wind Sailor			Edible Crab		
California Poppy			Edible Dulse		
California Sea Lion			Edible Sea Urchin		
Chameleon Prawn			test		
Channeled Wrack			Eel		
Clam Worm			Eel Grass		
Cockle			Flat Periwinkle		
Common Cerith			Flounder		
Common Cuttlefish			Fulmar		
cuttlebone			Gannet		
Common Grey Sea Slug			Great Black-backed Gull		
Common Hermit Crab			Greater Pipefish		
Common Limpet			Grey Seal		
Common Lobster			Gribble		
Common Mediterranean Sea Urchin			holes in driftwood		
Common Periwinkle			Guillemot		
Common Porpoise			Gut Laver		
Common Prawn			Harbor Seal		
			Hermit Crab Anemone		

	X	Date seen		X	Date seen
Keelworm			Sea Bindweed		
Kelp			Sea Campion		
Kittiwake			Sea Gooseberry		
Knotted Egg Wrack			Sea Holly		
Limacia clavigera			Sea Horse		
Lion's Mane Jellyfish			Sea Lace		
Lugworm cast			Sea Lavender		
Lumpsucker			Sea Lettuce		
Manx Shearwater			Sea Mouse		
Marram Grass			Sea Orange		
Moon Jellyfish			Sea Potato		
Mussel			test		
Necklace Shell			Sea Rocket		
Oyster			Sea Slater		
Oystercatcher			Sea Stickleback		
Painted Topshell			Shag		
Pelican			Shelduck		
Pelican's Foot Shell			Shore Crab		
Plated Lobster			Slender-legged Spider		
Plumose Anemone			Crab		
Porcelain Crab			Slipper Limpet		
Portuguese			Snakelocks Anemone		
Man-o'-War			Spider Stromb		
Puffin			Spiny Starfish		
Purple-tipped Sea Urchin			Sponge Crab		
Queen Scallop			Sunstar		
Ragwort			Thornback Spider		
Razor Shell			Crab		
Razorbill			Thrift		
Redshank			Toad Crab		
Ridged Abalone			Tompot Blenny		
Ringed Plover			Turnstone		
Rock Goby			Velvet Swimming Crab		
Sand Eel			White Clover		
Sanderling			Yellow Horned Poppy		
Sandhopper					
Saw Wrack					
Scorpion Fish					
Sea Aster					
Sea Belt					

Index

Additional illustrations by:
David Baxter, Andrew Beckett, Joyce Bee, Roland Berry, Trevor Boyer, Hilary Burn, Terry Callcut, Pete Dennis, Sandra Fernandez, Mike Freeman (photos), Victoria Gordon, Alan Harris, Bob Hersey, Christine Howes, Deborah King, Steven Kirk, Andy Martin, Annabel Milne, Patricia Mynott, David Nash, Gill Platt, David Quinn, John Shackell, Chris Shields, Peter Stebbing, George Thompson, Peter Warner, Phil Weare.

This book is based on material previously published in Usborne Spotter's Guides: *Fishes, Sea and Freshwater Birds, Seashore* and *Shells*; Usborne Nature Trail Books: *Birdwatching, Seashore Life* and *Wild Flowers*; Usborne Understanding Geography: *Seas and Oceans*; Usborne Science and Nature: *Ornithology*; Usborne Guide: *The Young Naturalist*; *The Great Animal Search*; *Usborne Mysteries and Marvels of Nature* and *The Usborne Living World Encyclopedia*.